The Sled

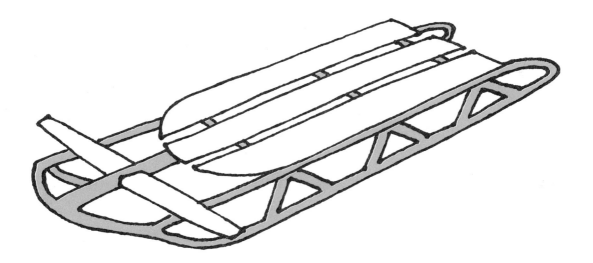

by Lynn Maslen Kertell
pictures by Sue Hendra

Scholastic Inc.
New York • Toronto • London • Auckland • Sydney • Mexico City • New Delhi • Hong Kong

Ask for Bob Books at your local bookstore, or visit www.bobbooks.com.

No part of this publication may be reproduced, stored in a retrieval system, or transmitted in any form, or by any means, electronic, mechanical, photocopying, recording, or otherwise, without written permission of the publisher. For information regarding permission, write to Scholastic Inc., Attention: Permissions Department, 557 Broadway, New York, NY 10012.

ISBN 978-0-545-34784-6

12 11 10 9 8 7 6 5 4 3 2 1   11 12 13 14 15/0

Printed in China / 68
This edition printing, January 2011

Mag had a sled.

"Will you sled with me?" said Mag.

"I will not sled with you,"
said the hen.

"Will you sled with me?" said Mag.

"I will not sled with you," said the frog.

"Will you sled with me?" said Mag.

"I will not sled with you," said the pig.

"I will sled with you," said Ruff.

Ruff will sled with Mag.

The End